Little Red Riding Hood

Key sound short oo spellings: o, oo, oul, u
Secondary sounds: ee, long oo, ou

Written by Nick Page
Illustrated by Clare Fennell

Reading with phonics

How to use this book

The **Reading with phonics** series helps you to have fun with your child and to support their learning of phonics and reading. It is aimed at children who have learned the letter sounds and are building confidence in their reading.

Each title in the series focuses on a different key sound. The entertaining retelling of the story repeats this sound frequently, and the different spellings for the sound are highlighted in red type. The first activity at the back of the book provides practice in reading and using words that contain this sound. The key sound for **Little Red Riding Hood** is the **short oo**.

Start by reading the story to your child, asking them to join in with the refrain in bold. Next, encourage them to read the story with you. Give them a hand to decode tricky words.

Now look at the activity pages at the back of the book. These are intended for you and your child to enjoy together. Most are not activities to complete in pencil or pen, but by reading and talking or pointing.

The **Key sound** pages focus on one sound, and on the various different groups of letters that produce that sound. Encourage your child to read the different letter groups and complete the activity, so they become more aware of the variety of spellings there are for the same sound.

The **Letters together** pages look at three pairs or groups of letters and at the sounds they make as they work together. Help your child to read the words and trace the route on the word maps.

Rhyme is used a lot in these retellings. Whatever stage your child has reached in their learning of phonics, it is always good practice for them to listen carefully for sounds and find words that rhyme. The pages on **Rhyming words** take six words from the story and ask children to read and find other words that rhyme with them.

The **Key words** pages focus on a number of key words that occur regularly but can nonetheless be challenging. Many of these words are not sounded out following the rules of phonics and the easiest thing is for children to learn them by sight, so that they do not worry about decoding them. These pages encourage children to retell the story, practising key words as they do so.

The **Picture dictionary** page asks children to focus closely on nine words from the story. Encourage children to look carefully at each word, cover it with their hand, write it on a separate piece of paper, and finally, check it!

Do not complete all the activities at once – doing one each time you read will ensure that your child continues to enjoy the stories and the time you are spending together. **Have fun!**

Here's a house, close to the wood.
Here's a girl who's kind and good.
Here's her favourite riding hood,
a gift from Grannie Annie.

In the woods, look out! Look out!
Could there be a wolf about?

"Grannie's ill," mum says, "so please,
be a good girl, take some cheese,
a book to read, some herbal teas
and pudding to your grannie."

In the woods, look out! Look out!
Could there be a wolf about?

Red set off across the brook.
A wolf looked on as she took
the herbal teas, the cheese, the book
and other goods to Grannie.

In the woods, look out! Look out!
Could there be a wolf about?

Wolf says, "Yum! I have a hunch,
by hook or crook, this could be lunch."
He runs ahead and with one "CRUNCH",
he swallows Grannie Annie.

Grannie's
House

In the woods, look out! Look out!
Could there be a wolf about?

Footsteps! Quick! Here comes Red.
Wolfie swiftly jumps in bed,
puts on Annie's clothes and says,
"Come and kiss your grannie!"

In the woods, look out! Look out!
Could there be a wolf about?

Red suspects a crooked plot.
"Grannie, what big ears you've got!"
"All the better to hear a lot,
now come and KISS your grannie!"

Grannie!

In the woods, look out! Look out!
Could there be a wolf about?

"Grannie, you've got such big eyes!"
"All the better to play I spy!"
(He's pulled the wool across her eyes.)
"Now COME AND KISS your grannie!"

Grannie!

In the woods, look out! Look out!
Could there be a wolf about?

Little Red, she shook with fear:
"What big teeth you have! Oh, dear!"
"Better to eat you! Now, come here,
BECAUSE I'M THE WOLF –
NOT GRANNIE!"

Oh, dear!

In the woods, look out! Look out!
Could there be a wolf about?

A lumberjack was passing through.
He heard the scream, knew what to do,
rushed in and chopped the wolf in two,
and out popped Grannie Annie!

In the woods, look out! Look out!
Could there be a wolf about?

Grannie!

So ends the book of Riding Hood.
We hope it's clearly understood:
you must be careful in the wood
and please be good to Grannie!

In the woods, look out! Look out!
Could there be a wolf about?

Key sound

There are several different groups of letters that make the **short oo** sound. Practise them by looking at the words in Little Red's baskets and using them to make sentences. Can you use each word in a different sentence?

wood   good   book

hood   crooked   look

brook   took   hook

goods   stood   wool

shook   wool

understood

wolf
woman

could
should
would

pudding
bull
put
butcher
pull
full
cushion

25

Letters together

Look at these pairs of letters and say
the sounds they make.

ee   oo   ou

Follow the words that contain *ee*
to see Grannie's big teeth.

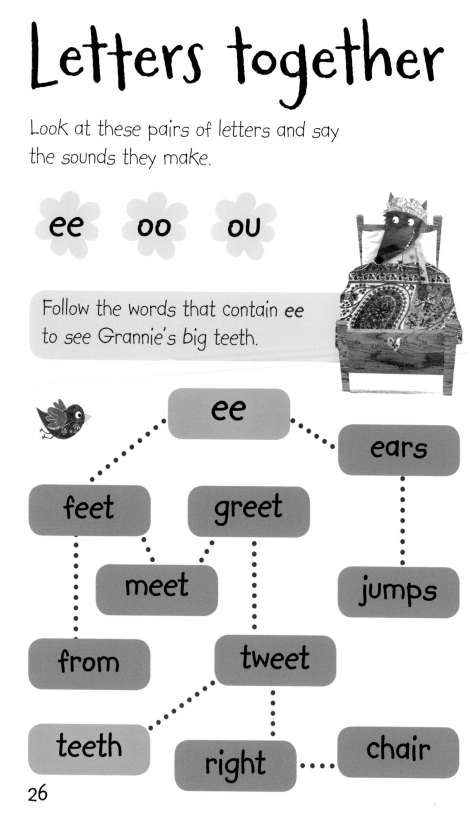

ee

ears

feet

greet

meet

jumps

from

tweet

teeth

right

chair

Follow the words that contain the **long oo** to help Little Red get some food.

oo

the

noon

moon tool

room · · · · soon other

pool **food** lots

Follow the words that contain **ou** to help Grannie out of the wolf.

about **ou**

shout

trout beautiful

other

mocks out

spout

27

Rhyming words

Read the words in the flowers and point to other words that rhyme with them.

wolf	cook
brook	tea

book

bed	near
teeth	fear

hear

kiss	hood
red	fed

bed

flea   **tea**   goods

cheese   sea

swallows   dream

scream

cream   runs

wood   grannie

hood

good   mum

Now choose a word and
make up a rhyming chant!

Should I wear
my **good hood** in
the **wood**?

Key words

Many common words can be tricky to sound out Practise them by reading these sentences about the story. Now make more sentences using other key words from around the border.

Little Red's mum told her to **go** to see her grannie.

Red saw it was **the** wolf, not grannie!

Red took **some** food to Grannie Annie.

There was a wolf watching Little Red.

Grannie **lived** in the woods.

not • found • into

• morning • different • took • looked • had • there • wit

The wolf went **into** Grannie Annie's house.

The wolf **put** on grannie's clothes.

The wolf **had** very big eyes.

The lumberjack knew what to **do.**

The wolf had **big** ears.

bed • lived • clothes • mother • was • her • put • jumped • door • come • and • food •

go • inside • trees • do • some • round • big • things

Picture dictionary

Look carefully at the pictures and the words.
Now cover the words, one at a time. Can you
remember how to write them?

book   brook   cheese

ears   girl   grannie

hood   lumberjack   teeth